Enid Blyton's
ENCHANTED WORLD
Petal and the Eternal Bloom

Elise Allen

EGMONT

Meet the
Faraway Fairies

Favourite Colour – Yellow. It's a beautiful colour that reminds me of sunshine and happiness.

Talent – Light. I can release rays of energy to light up a room or, if I really try hard, I can use it to break out of tight situations. The only problem is that when I lose my temper I can have a 'flash attack' which is really embarrassing because my friends find it funny.

Favourite Activity – Exploring. I love an adventure, even when it gets me into trouble. I never get tired of visiting new places and meeting new people.

Favourite Colour – Blue. The colour of the sea and the sky. I love every shade from aquamarine to midnight blue.

Talent – As well as being a musician I can also transform into other objects. I like to do it for fun, but it also comes in useful if there's a spot of bother.

Favourite Activity – Singing and dancing. I can do it all day and never get tired.

Favourite Colour – Green. It's the colour of life. All my best plant friends are one shade of green or another.

Talent – I can speak to the animals and plants of the Enchanted World . . . not to mention the ones in the Faraway Tree.

Favourite Activity – I love to sit peacefully and listen to the constant chatter of all creatures, both big and small.

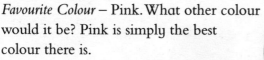

Favourite Colour – Pink. What other colour would it be? Pink is simply the best colour there is.

Talent – Apart from being a supreme fashion designer, I can also become invisible. It helps me to escape from my screaming fashion fans!

Favourite Activity – Designing. Give me some fabrics and I'll make you something fabulous. Remember – If it's not by Pinx . . . your makeover stinks!

Favourite Colour – Orange. It's the most fun colour of all. It's just bursting with life!

Talent – Being a magician of course. Although I have been known to make the odd Basic Bizzy Blunder with my spells.

Favourite Activity – Baking Brilliant Blueberry Buns and Marvellous Magical Muffins. There is always time to bake a tasty cake to show your friends that you care.

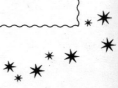

www.blyton.com/enchantedworld

Contents

Introduction

*T*ucked away among the thickets, groves and
forests of our Earth is a special wood. An
Enchanted Wood, where the trees grow taller, the
branches grow stronger and the leaves grow denser
than anywhere else. Search hard enough within this
Enchanted Wood, and you'll find one tree that
towers above all the others. This is the Faraway Tree,
and it is very special. It is home to magical creatures
like elves and fairies, even a dragon. But the most
magical thing about this very magical Tree? It is the
sole doorway to the Lands of the Enchanted World.

Most of the time, the Lands of the Enchanted
World simply float along, unattached to anything.
But at one time or another, they each come to rest at

the top of the Faraway Tree. And if you're lucky enough to be in the Tree at the time, you can climb to its very top, scramble up the long Ladder extending from its tallest branch, push through the clouds and step into that Land.

Of course, there's no telling when a Land will come to the Faraway Tree, or how long it will remain. A Land might stay for months, or be gone within the hour. And if you haven't made it back down the Ladder and into the Faraway Tree before the Land floats away, you could be stuck for a very long time. This is scary even in the most wonderful of Lands, like the Land of Perfect Birthday Parties. But if you get caught in a place like the Land of Ravenous Toothy Beasts, the situation is absolutely terrifying. Yet even though exploring the Lands has its perils, it's also exhilarating, which is why creatures from all over the Enchanted World (and the occasional visiting human) come to live in the Faraway Tree so they can travel from Land to Land.

Of course, not everyone explores the Lands for

pleasure alone. In fact, five fairies have been asked
do so for the ultimate cause: to save the life of the
Faraway Tree and make sure the doorway to the
Enchanted World remains open. These are their
stories . . .

Chapter One

Petal's Room

'Oh honestly, you are impossible,' Petal scolded.

Every other bird, squirrel, chipmunk and tree frog in Petal's room waited its turn for the breakfast crumbs she gave them, but not the raven. The minute he got the chance, he swooped down, pushed everyone else out of the way and devoured as many morsels as possible, triggering screeching protests from the other creatures in the room.

'Enough!' Petal cried. 'Have I ever let any of you miss breakfast?'

One of the difficulties of talking to plants and animals was the noise. Petal's ears buzzed constantly with all kinds of chatter: magpies and starlings nattering about the places they had flown; vines fighting over who was the longest; and diva blooms which clucked in annoyance at anything *daring* to look as beautiful as them.

At times like these, Petal was grateful that she could not read their minds. The very idea of adding their twittering thoughts to the babble of conversation that she could already hear gave her a headache.

'Petal! I need you!' Pinx cried as she soared in from above.

Petal's room had only three walls; the fourth wall and ceiling were wide open to nature, allowing a constant stream of creatures – as well as Petal's fairy friends – to flutter, crawl and skitter in and out.

Pinx was holding a piece of fabric, talking at top speed and poring over the blossoms in Petal's room.

'I was out there trying to make the most fantabulacious sash that just screamed,

"WOW!" and it wasn't screaming at all, it was whimpering, and clearly a Pinx sash *cannot* whimper, and then BOOM! it came to me exactly what it needs: flowers! And where can I find the best flowers?' Pinx's eyes widened as she came to a fuzzy, orange-leafed bush with giant blooms bursting with fuchsia and teal. '*Here*!' she cried, and began plucking flowers as quickly as she could.

Petal winced as the bush (whose name was Imogene) gave a shrill scream.

'You tell that fairy she has no right to pick my blooms without asking first! Maybe we should see how she likes it when I snag my thorn on one of her silly dresses!'

'This is perfect, Petal!' Pinx cried. 'Thanks – you're the best!'

'*You're* the best?' Imogene spluttered. 'Did *you* raise thirty-seven flowers from bud to bloom? Did *you* –'

'No, *you* did, Imogene,' said Petal, 'and if

you hadn't done such a spectacular job, Pinx wouldn't want your flowers at all. If you ask me, it's a compliment.'

Petal smiled as Imogene stammered, unable to argue with this logic. But her satisfaction was immediately interrupted by . . .

'Petal, prepare for a Piece of Prestidigitation of Preposterously Prodigious Proportions!' Bizzy cried as she flew in.

'What does *that* mean?' Petal asked.

'I have a great new spell!' Bizzy translated, raising her arms with a flourish and making all her bangles rattle. 'Watch as I turn this patch of small flowers into Titanic Towers of Treelike Treasures!'

Bizzy saw Petal's confused look and explained, 'I'm going to make them taller!'

A look of doubt crossed Petal's face.

'That is, if you think they won't mind,' Bizzy added.

'Mind?' a flower cried. 'We'd *love* to be taller!'

The whole patch clamoured for Bizzy to get on with her spell immediately.

'Go for it,' Petal said.

Bizzy closed her eyes, concentrated and then cried, 'Flahwahh-groo, flahwahh-graa, flahwahh-groodle-oodle-grow!'

'AAAAAHHHHH!' came the horrified screams of thirty blooms.

'Hmmm,' Bizzy winced, looking at her handiwork. 'I don't think I got the spell quite right. Instead of "taller", the flowers got . . .'

'*Teal*er!' the flowers wailed.

The previously yellow blossoms were now a bright shade of greenish-blue that made them look more sickly than beautiful.

'Oh no, here we go again,' sighed a rose.

Petal turned and saw Melody flying in. Melody knew that plants liked music, and she often sang to them. Unfortunately, Melody didn't realise that certain lilies and roses were very particular about the *volume* of the music.

'Can't someone turn her down?' huffed a lily.

'Oh, no!' came a sudden cry from the daffodils.

Silky was flying towards them. Silky adored daffodils, but she had a habit of putting her whole nose deep inside the bloom to inhale its scent . . .

'Hasn't she ever heard of personal space?' cried Daffo, one of the taller blooms.

Petal laughed as she hovered in the middle of her room, surrounded by the squeals of the plants, the background chatter of the animals and the voices of her friends. Life in the Faraway Tree was never dull for a second. It didn't matter to her that there was always a dilemma or an argument taking place somewhere. She was happy to let it all wash over her. It was her ability to remain serene, calm and loyal that made everybody in the Faraway Tree love her.

'AH . . . AH . . . *ACHOOO*!'

The wind from the sneeze blew several of Imogene's blooms off Pinx's sash.

'My sash!' Pinx cried, zooming into the air with her hands on her hips. 'Whoever did this has about five seconds to confess!'

A giant nose peeked out from between several stalks of bamboo.

'Sorry,' Cluecatcher said as he pushed his way into the room. 'I'm allergic to bamboo.'

Witch Whisper was behind Cluecatcher, and the sight of them made Petal suddenly attentive because she knew . . .

'There's a new land at the top of the Tree!' Silky cried.

'Yes,' Witch Whisper confirmed, 'and it's one in which your help, Petal, will be very important.'

'*Me*?' Petal asked.

'It's the Land of Flora,' Cluecatcher said. 'It's populated solely by plants.'

'A Positively Perfect Petal Place!' Bizzy grinned.

'The Talisman there is the Eternal Bloom,' Witch Whisper continued, 'a beautiful flower that never wilts. You need to bring it back to the Vault before the Land moves away from the Tree . . . and before Talon finds it.'

'Assuming Talon ever escaped the didgeridoo in the Land of Music,' Melody giggled.

The other Fairies giggled too . . . until they noticed Witch Whisper frowning at them.

'Talon is stronger than you think,' she said. 'You have had success against him, but each success only makes him angrier. He feeds on that fury, and grows more powerful every time. I warn you not to underestimate him . . . or it could be your undoing.'

Witch Whisper smiled and looked into the eyes of each fairy. They could all see the confidence that burned there. Despite her warnings, she had faith that they could succeed.

'You must get ready,' she said. 'As soon as The Land of Flora settles at the top of the Tree, Talon will start searching for the Eternal Bloom.'

Although Talon did not enter Lands by the Faraway Tree's Ladder, his magical transportation abilities were very limited. He could only magic himself into a Land that had stopped moving, and there was only one thing that could attach itself to a Land and make it stop – the Faraway Tree.

'So . . . are you ready?' Witch Whisper asked.

Petal thought about the Land of Flora. It was exactly the kind of place that she had dreamed of visiting when Silky first told her about the mission, and she felt a shiver of excitement race through her body. She beamed at Witch Whisper.

'I can't wait,' she said.

Chapter Two

An Explosion of Colour

At Silky's request, Petal led the fairies up the Ladder to the Land of Flora. She climbed steadily through the light cloud that always nestled at the top of the tree until finally she burst out of the top of the cloud and into an explosion of red confetti. The bright, puffy specks danced and swirled around the fairies in a bubble of colour.

'It's snowing red!' Melody giggled.

'I don't think it's snow . . .' Silky mused.

She was right. It wasn't confetti either. It was . . .

'Dandelion fluff!' Petal cried joyfully.

'*Red* dandelion fluff?' Pinx asked, amazed.

'And blue!' Bizzy exclaimed, pointing. 'And yellow! And orange!'

Sure enough, all around the fairies, multicoloured dandelions were shooting balls of fluff into the air, where they exploded in glorious spheres of dancing seeds in every colour of the rainbow.

'It's like fireworks!' Melody marvelled.

Petal had been so amazed by the fluff that she hadn't paid attention to the hum of strange new voices in her head. After all, she was used to constant background chatter from the plants at home. But this was different, and as she listened, she burst into a huge smile.

'It *is* just like fireworks,' she confirmed. 'The plants are celebrating our arrival! Look!'

The fairies looked beyond the swirls of fluff to an ocean of flowering plants in every shape and size. There wasn't an inch of bare soil. Giant purple-and-pink-polka-dotted sunflowers were pressed against sprawling candy-striped daisies; sprays of dazzlingly bright snapdragons reached up to vivid umbrellas of dangling bluebells; and on and on and on, as far as the eye could see. Many of the plants bobbed happily back and forth, and Melody had the feeling that they were ...

'Dancing!' she squealed. 'They're dancing, aren't they?'

'They are!' Petal confirmed, beaming. 'They're singing, too, about how happy they are to have company.'

But the plants didn't want to dance by themselves.

'Whooooaaa!' cried the fairies as they were each scooped into the stems of several of the largest flowers, and twirled and swirled among them in time to their music.

Petal was the only one who could hear their song, but Melody could tell the beat from the dancing rhythm and she joined in with her own happy chorus.

'Aaahhh!' Bizzy giggled, as her dance

partner threw her on to a massive, sprawling flower with a soft purple middle that sprang her into the air like a giant trampoline. 'Look at me! I'm on a Brilliantly Bouncy Bloom!'

'I want to do it too!' cried Silky.

She and Petal leaped on to the trampoline with Bizzy, flipping, twirling and flopping as their new plant friends clapped their leaves together with glee. It felt like a carnival: the dandelion-fluff fireworks, the candy-coloured flowers, the trampoline, Melody and the plants' giddy tune, and Pinx swinging high above on a blossom suspended between two plants.

'This is great!' Pinx whooped as she soared high on her swing. 'Who knew plants could be this much fun!'

'*I* did!' Petal retorted.

'They're Fantastically Flowerrific!' Bizzy shouted as she did a perfect double flip.

'And Positively Plantastic?' added Melody with a shy smile.

'YES!' Bizzy cried merrily.

Silky grabbed Petal's hands and they bounced together, higher and higher, their grins stretching their faces.

'Petal,' Silky shouted over the air rushing past their ears as they bounced, 'do the plants know where we can find the Eternal Bloom?'

'I don't know . . . let me ask them,' said Petal.

She released Silky's hands mid-jump and flew high into the air. 'Anyone who can hear me,' she cried, 'I'm looking for a flower called the Eternal Bloom! If anyone knows, please tell me where I can find the Bloom; it's really important for the entire Enchanted World!'

Petal hovered in mid-air, straining to hear any sound. The other fairies strained as well, although they knew they wouldn't understand the answer even if it came. Several long minutes ticked by. Then a slight breeze ruffled the plants nearby and Petal grinned.

'Thank you!' she shouted excitedly into the distance. 'Thank you very much!'

She flitted back down to her friends.

'They've seen her!' she cried. 'The Bloom is in the Fields of Fancy!'

'The Fabulous Fields of Fancy?' Bizzy asked. 'Sounds fun! Let's fly!'

'We can't,' Petal said. 'The plants are saying it could take days.' Her mouth spread into a smile and she nodded at a huge yellow-and-blue-polka-dotted blossom that was unfurling one of its petals like a giant tongue. 'But he says he can get us there in no time if we just climb on.'

'Let's do it then,' Silky agreed.

She threw her arms around the nearest group of stems and hugged them tightly.

'Thank you all for a perfect welcome,' she called out to all the plants and flowers. 'It was wonderful to meet you.'

The other fairies gave hugs and called out goodbyes as well. Then they climbed on to the enormous petal of the yellow-and-blue blossom and held on tight as the petal bent back … back … back …

'Um, Petal?' Melody said, as the petal stretched impossibly far backwards and the fairies clutched it tightly to stay aboard. 'Are you sure this is a good idea?'

'What do you mean?' Petal asked.

Melody gave a nervous shrug. 'I was just wondering if we might end up flying too faAAAAAAA!'

She never got to finish her sentence. The petal flicked forwards, catapulting the fairies through the sky at super speed and leaving their new plant friends with nothing but the trailing sound of their screams as they rocketed away.

Chapter Three

The Fields of Fancy

None of the fairies had ever moved this fast or felt so out of control. They screamed as the wind whipped back their hair and plastered their wings to their backs. Melody screwed up her eyes, too nervous to look.

'Just tell me when we've landed, OK?' she gasped.

'Oh Melody, no – you have to see!' Petal cried. 'It's beautiful!'

It was more than beautiful. For Petal, soaring over the Land of Flora was absolutely heavenly. As she and her friends zipped across the sky, a universe of trees, leaves, flowers and every kind of foliage imaginable whizzed below them. At their speed, the landscape changed so quickly that it made Petal dizzy.

Rainforests of giant ferns were followed by a deep gorge with dazzling waterfalls. Moments later, the ground was dry and desert cacti reached out to the fairies. Within seconds, that gave way to an array of tiny, speckled flowers in every colour imaginable. Petal longed to explore this fabulous land in all its glory.

Eventually the fairies slowed down and their wings were again free to move. They fluttered down and landed on a thick branch.

'I think we've found the Fields of Fancy,' grinned Pinx, gazing around.

Every branch, vine and stem grew in long curls and swirls, with leaves like pieces of lace. Giant flowers bloomed in rich reds and pinks, growing in textures the fairies had never before seen in nature: feathers, sequinelles, bubbloons, taffetellas ... if there could possibly be a fancier field, none of them could imagine it.

'I love it!' Pinx declared.

'Of course you love it!' Silky laughed. 'It

looks as if your wardrobe exploded and planted itself!'

'Oh, look!' Melody cooed. 'The plants are coming to introduce themselves!'

Sure enough, a group of twisting vines covered with fluffy flowers had stretched towards the fairies.

'Hi,' said Melody, reaching out to a tiny baby blossom exactly at her eye level. 'You're such a sweet little –'

But before she could reach out to caress the bloom, all the vines leaped forwards and lashed their tendrils around the fairies, snatching them high into the air.

'Hey!' screamed Pinx.

One vine held her tight while another poked at her face, her pigtails and her necklace.

'*Hey!*' she yelled again. 'Hands off my stuff.'

She kicked and squirmed, but she couldn't escape the vine's grasp.

'Um . . . Petal?' Bizzy said, her voice
wavering as another vine shook her up and
down. 'If this is Flower Fun, it's Frighteningly
Forceful.'

'Oof,' was Petal's only immediate response.

Her vine had just grabbed Melody and
Silky, and snapped them all closely together
like a bouquet. The vine then raised the
threesome to the centre of a blossom, which
leaned down to . . . *smell* them.

'What's happening?' asked Silky.

'They've never seen fairies before,' said Petal. 'They don't realise that we're living creatures. They think we're just pretty things to play with.'

A vine plucked Melody from the bouquet and tucked her tightly between two petals of a giant blossom, which preened to show off its new decoration.

'Maybe you can just tell them nicely that we're actually individuals with thoughts and feelings,' Melody suggested to Petal.

'I've *been* telling them,' Petal said, 'but it's not working.'

Although they hadn't heard Petal's pleas, the other fairies knew that she was telling the truth, having learned long ago that Petal could direct thoughts as well as speech at plants and animals.

'But you're fluent in flower!' Bizzy cried, who was now being dangled upside down from her ankles while smaller tendrils dashed playfully back and forth through her cascading curls.

'They hear me, but it doesn't mean they'll listen!' said Petal.

'Then let's stop asking and *tell* them to let us go!' Pinx screamed. 'Here's the plan: Silky shoots them with a beam of light; Bizzy magics up a lawnmower and Melody turns into a really hungry goat! Go!'

'No!' Petal gasped. 'No goats! No magic, no light beams. The plants aren't being nasty; they just don't know any better. In fact, if you think about it, they're only treating us the way most of us usually treat them. At least they're not actually hurting us; we pick flowers apart to play "loves me, loves me not"!'

Petal spoke before she realised the effect her words might have. There was a sudden silence among the vines . . . and then they gathered the five fairies into one giant bunch and started tugging to see which parts would come loose.

'Hey!' shouted Silky as a vine took away her tiara.

'Oh!' cried Melody as another vine grabbed her shoes.

'Ow!' yelped Pinx as a vine yanked one of her pigtails. 'That's attached!' But the vine just yanked it again, harder. '*OW!*'

The vines seemed puzzled that they couldn't grab Pinx's hair as easily as the shoes and tiara. Two vines snaked themselves firmly around each of Pinx's lightning-bolt-shaped pigtails, preparing to pull with all their might.

'Petal!' shrieked Pinx. 'We need to do something *NOW!*'

Chapter Four

The Eternal Bloom

Pinx winced, positive that the next thing she would feel would be her hair ripping out of her head. But just as the vines seemed to be about to give a final, massive tug, they released the fairies and backed away sheepishly. One came back briefly to put Silky's tiara back on her head (backwards) and Melody's shoes back on her feet (mixing up right and left), and then it hurried away.

'Thank you,' Petal said, bowing low.

She was facing away from the tormenting vines. Silky, Bizzy, Pinx and Melody followed her gaze and saw the largest, thickest, lushest vine yet. An elegant leaf unfurled from its very tip, and on that leaf perched a small but almost impossibly perfect red blossom.

'It's beautiful,' Melody gasped.

'It's so tiny,' Bizzy added.

'It would look so pretty on my sash!' Pinx crowed.

She tried to fly up to pluck the blossom, but Silky held her back.

'I don't think so, Pinx,' Silky smiled. 'That's the Eternal Bloom.'

Silky held up her crystal necklace for her

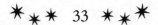

friends to see: it was glowing bright red.

'So the *Talisman* rescued *us*!' Bizzy laughed. Maybe we're actually in the Land of Inside-Out and Backwards. Now Talon will come and throw us all a party with a Colossal Coconut Congratulations Cake!'

Melody gave a giggle. 'This is our easiest mission yet!'

'It will be once we get out of here,' Pinx grumbled. 'I don't trust these plants.'

She whipped her head around and glared at one of the vines, which had been sneaking closer and closer to her irresistible pigtails. It backed off again.

'You're right,' Silky agreed.

She moved forward to where Petal was standing close to the Eternal Bloom, looking serious and nodding frequently.

'Excuse me,' Silky said, remembering Petal's low bow and giving a little curtsy. 'Thank you for saving us, Eternal Bloom. I hate to interrupt your conversation, but we need to get you back to the Vault right away.'

The Bloom seemed to shiver, and Petal soothed it with a gentle hand.

'I'll handle this,' she said softly to the flower.

She flew off a short distance, motioning for the other fairies to follow her.

'What's up?' Pinx asked. 'Why didn't you grab the flower?'

Petal frowned.

'We have a bit of a problem,' she said. 'The Eternal Bloom doesn't want to go back to the Vault.'

Pinx cocked her head to one side.

'The plant?' she said in a matter-of-fact tone. 'The *plant* doesn't want to go back to the Vault?'

'Exactly,' Petal agreed. 'She says that she feels too confined there, and –'

'And why should we care about this?' Pinx exploded. 'She's a *plant*! She doesn't get a say!'

Silky shot Pinx a look that silenced her and then turned back to Petal, who was clearly upset.

'Tell us, Petal,' she said.

'The Bloom is a living creature,' Petal said. 'She doesn't like being shut up in a Vault every day with nothing to do but sit and stare at the walls. Would you?'

'I wouldn't,' Melody said softly.

'Exactly,' continued Petal. 'But that's all the Bloom has ever done. Now she's finally living free in the Land of Flora, she's happy for the first time ever and she doesn't want to give it up.'

'I understand that,' Silky said. 'But the Tree needs the energy from the Talismans in the Vault to survive.'

'And if we don't take her back, how do we know Talon won't come and get her?' Bizzy added. 'If he does, he's connected to the Land of Flora – he can take it over.'

'I know. I know all of that,' Petal said. 'But I also know that we can't take the Bloom against her will.'

'Of course we can!' Pinx burst. 'She's small – we just pick her up and go. Watch!'

Pinx lunged for the Bloom, but Petal shouted, 'Stop her!' to a nearby vine. Delighted, the vine leaped forwards and

wrapped itself around Pinx, securing her tightly as she kicked and struggled.

'Petal!' spluttered Pinx.

'I'm not going to let you kidnap her!' said Petal.

As they argued, Melody looked more and more pained. She hated it when her friends fought and she kept trying to jump in and break it up, but Pinx and Petal ignored her.

'Help me,' Melody begged Bizzy. 'Do a spell – something to distract them!'

'I know the perfect thing: a clown!' said Bizzy.

She closed her eyes to concentrate and then sang out: 'Cliddle-clee-cliddle-oh-cliddle-cloo!'

A tiny, puffy, white cloud appeared between Melody and Bizzy. The two fairies just looked at it.

'It's sweet . . .' Bizzy said.

Petal and Pinx were still screaming at each

other and Silky couldn't bear it for one more second. The sight of Petal, who was normally so quiet and composed, shouting back at Pinx as if her life depended on it was something that frightened Silky.

'Both of you stop this right now,' she wailed.

The volume was getting unbearable. Silky felt an angry rush of heat flood her face and explode into a powerful beam of light that smacked against the vine, causing it to drop Pinx.

'Right,' said Silky, as Pinx picked herself up off the ground. 'Now can we talk about this like civilised fairies? I think we should get her safely to the Tree and have a talk. If she really understands what's at stake, I'm sure she'll go back to the Vault.'

'And we can make the Vault so much nicer for her!' Melody said excitedly. 'We can pipe music in there, and maybe come down and perform plays or dances . . . then she'd never get bored!'

'Or I could magic up some Flower Friends for her,' Bizzy offered. 'Then she would be happy all the time, no matter what!'

'*Or* we could just follow our mission and put her in the Vault, like we do with all the other Talismans,' Pinx said.

'Pinx, we're trying to come up with a solution that works for *everyone*,' said Silky. 'What do you think, Petal?'

Silky turned to her . . . but she wasn't there. When had she slipped away from the group?

'Petal?' Silky called, looking all around, 'Petal?'

'It's not just her,' Melody realised. 'Look.'

She pointed to the leaf where the Eternal Bloom had perched. It had gone too. Silky quickly grabbed her crystal necklace and held it up to her face. It was perfectly clear. Petal and the Eternal Bloom had gone.

Chapter Five

The Friends Separated

'Wheeeeee!'

The Eternal Bloom giggled and squealed. She had never flown before, and now she was speeding through the air, the wind whipping through her petals.

'Look at me, look at me, look at me, I'm *flying*!' the Bloom cried, her words ringing in Petal's ears. 'I'm soaring and sailing and zipping and zooming and oh Petal, it's absolutely *glorious*!'

'Glorious' wouldn't have been Petal's choice of words. She still couldn't believe that she had abandoned her four best friends in a Land where they didn't know the language . . .

Petal shook her head to dislodge those thoughts. Her friends were brilliant; they

could handle the Land of Flora. She hadn't
planned to leave them, but she had just been
so upset by their talk of snatching the Bloom
and stuffing her into the Vault against her
will. The very idea sickened Petal, and before
she could even think about what she was
doing, she had pocketed the Bloom and asked
a large plant to catapult the two of them as
far away as possible.

They were flying through a new part of the

Land of Flora, where the trees sprouted no flowers or leaves – only spines and thorns that grew together to make a sharp mesh, guaranteed to shred anything that dared cross its path.

'Go away!' the spiny trees bellowed in deep, gravelly voices. 'We don't want you here! Turn away and don't come back!'

Petal didn't want to anger the trees. She was about to turn away when the Bloom's voice rang out.

'Poppycock!' she cried. 'Petal and the Eternal Bloom would like to go through. Out of the way, thorns! Make way!'

'The Eternal Bloom?'

'Hmmm . . .'

'Well, that's different . . .'

A chorus of grumbling rang through the thorny woods, and then the trees parted their thorns in a circular tunnel just big enough for Petal to fly through.

'Thank you,' Petal said.

The Bloom bowed in thanks as they flew into the tunnel. It was dark and snug, and it closed up behind Petal as she flew, making her feel as if it would swallow her alive if she didn't move quickly enough. The Bloom didn't have the same concerns.

'Isn't it dark and spooky in here?' she said. 'I love it! I feel like we should tell ghost stories. Do you know any ghost stories? Oh, I'm so thrilled you're here with me! Exploring on my own was delightful, but to share it all with a friend . . . it's more marvellous than I ever could have dreamed!'

'I like being with you, too,' Petal said with a smile.

Petal soared out through the end of the tunnel and looked over her shoulder to watch the wall of thorns and spines close in on itself, as if the opening had never been there. Unfortunately, looking backwards meant that she wasn't looking forwards . . .

'Look out!' the Bloom screeched.

Petal whipped her head around just in time to see a giant black-and-white-striped plant towering in front of them. She tried to stop, but she was flying too quickly and she bumped into the fuzzy stalk. The enormous plant screamed – a high-pitched wail that hurt Petal's ears – and released a purple cloud of mist from its top. As the mist fell towards Petal and the Bloom, they smelled a stench that was so hideous, it almost made them pass out.

'AAARGH!' they screamed together.

Petal flew away as fast as she could, barely watching where she was going. She had never seen a Mephitis plant before, but their powers were the stuff of legend. The mist that the flowers had sprayed in all directions was a powerful combination of the smell of rotten eggs, mouldy cheese and unwashed feet. If you were unfortunate enough to have even a drop land on you, you would reek of the

hideous scent for seven years, and no amount
of baths or perfumes could cover it up.

Petal flew at top speed until her breath
rasped out in heavy pants and she didn't have
the energy to move another muscle. She
plopped down on a cushy-looking flower and
took the Eternal Bloom from her pocket,
holding her up to eye level.

'That was close,' Petal said. 'Smell anything on me?'

'Not a thing,' said the Bloom. 'On me?'

Petal inhaled deeply and smelled nothing but the Bloom's natural flowery aroma.

'No,' she said.

Petal and the Bloom looked at one another for a moment . . . and then burst into hysterical laughter.

'Oh Petal,' the Bloom said, 'if you could have seen your face!'

'What did you think my face would look like?' Petal retorted. 'You really think I want to spend seven years smelling like *cheesy feet*?'

The very idea reduced them both to hysterics again, and they laughed until they were exhausted. As the last giggles left them, Petal lay back on their flowery perch and looked at the Bloom. The more she looked, the more thoughtful she grew, and her smile started to fade.

'What?' asked the Bloom.

'It must have been horrible for you in the Vault,' said Petal.

The Bloom considered.

'Not horrible,' she replied. 'It had been so long since I'd known anything else. But now that I do, the idea of going back there . . .'

She shuddered, and Petal soothed her with a reassuring hand.

'I won't let that happen,' Petal promised.

'You say that so easily . . . but I know you left your friends for me,' said the Bloom. 'I don't believe that was easy for you at all.'

'No,' agreed Petal, 'but it was the right thing to do. I couldn't let them take you against your will.'

Petal sounded firm, but her mind was filled with doubt. Of course saving the Bloom had been right, but if she'd given her friends more time and not raced off in the heat of the moment, maybe she could have convinced

them to help her. And yet if she hadn't . . .
could she have forgiven herself if the Bloom
ended up miserable back in the Vault?

No – Petal wouldn't allow herself to turn it
over in her mind any more. She had made her
decision; she was protecting the Bloom. One
less Talisman in the Vault wouldn't destroy the
Faraway Tree.

'I won't let my friends take you back, but I
can't let Talon take you either,' she said.

'Talon?' asked the Bloom.

Petal told her all about the evil Troll.

'So we just have to find a safe place to hide
you,' she finished. 'Come on.'

Petal scooped the Bloom back into her
pocket and flew upwards.

'Oh my,' Petal breathed, as she gazed out
over the near-perfect landscape.

She hadn't noticed it when they were
racing away from the Mephitis plant, but now
it took her breath away. Lush, green hills and

valleys spread as far as the eye could see. In the middle of it all was a stunning waterfall, roaring as it crashed down to the river below. Petal grinned as she noticed a cave near the waterfall's top.

'There,' she said.

When Petal reached the cave, she knew that she had found the perfect hideout. It was huge, stretching back farther than Petal could see. Thick, soft grass carpeted the ground and fuzzy moss covered the walls. Berries grew in ripe, round clumps along the sides of the cave, and the river could provide all the water they would need.

'What do you think?' Petal asked.

'It's lovely,' the Bloom replied uncertainly, peering out of Petal's pocket. 'But I'd get awfully frightened and worried if I had to stay here alone. And I don't know how I'd ever know when it was safe to come out. And I certainly couldn't –'

'It's OK,' Petal soothed her. 'I'll stay with you until it's safe. I promise.'

'Thank you,' said the Bloom.

She yawned and quickly fell asleep.

Petal couldn't imagine napping when so much was on her mind . . . and yet the cave was so very cosy, and the light inside was so soothingly dim . . . and she was awfully tired from flying so fast and so far . . .

Within moments Petal too was asleep, comfortably cocooned in the snug little den.

But Petal and the Bloom weren't the only ones to have discovered the cave. Someone else had arrived before them and, as they rested, that someone was licking his wicked lips in anticipation and marvelling at his good luck.

Chapter Six

A Friend in Need

'I can't believe she left us,' Bizzy said. They were all stunned and could only stare at the spot where the Bloom had last been.

'Yes,' Pinx laughed. 'I didn't know she had it in her.'

'It's not funny!' Melody snapped.

Bizzy, Pinx and Silky spun to face her, surprised by the anger in her voice.

'I know it's not *really* funny,' Pinx amended. 'I'm just saying, she must have been really upset . . .'

'I don't care how upset she was,' Melody insisted. 'You don't leave your friends. You just don't!'

Pinx and Bizzy exchanged looks. They had

never seen Melody like this, and they didn't know what to say. Silky, however, flew to Melody and put an arm around her shoulders.

'It's not that she doesn't love us, Melody,' Silky soothed her friend. 'I think she didn't know how else to save the Bloom. She's the most loyal person in the whole Enchanted World, so to leave us must mean that she felt as if she had no other choice.'

'Maybe we should have just listened to Petal and let the Bloom go,' Melody said softly, the anger draining from her voice. 'One missing Talisman wouldn't be so awful for the Tree, would it?'

'*Now* you tell me! What about when I needed the Rainbow Feather for Princess Twilleria's Sweet Centennial gown?' Pinx cried.

'She *had* the Feather on her gown,' Silky reminded her. 'Talon's the one who took it away.'

'But Pinx is right,' Bizzy added. 'What if the Rainbow Feather was scared of leaving Fairyland? What if the Enchanted Harp wanted to stay in the Land of Music? What if we listened to every Talisman and the Vault stayed empty? What if – MMMMPPPH!'

Two vines had grabbed Bizzy, one twisting itself around her mouth and the other twining around her waist. They hoisted her high into the air, Bizzy's arms and legs flailing all the way.

'Bizzy!' Silky shouted.

Then she screamed as a vine wound its way around her own ankle and yanked her upside down. Vines weaved themselves through Pinx's pigtails and up and down Melody's arms. With the Bloom gone, the vines could go back to playing with the fairies, and now it looked as if Melody, Silky, Pinx and Bizzy would be torn apart!

'*NO!*' Silky shouted. 'Not again!'

Anger seared through her body and powerful rays of light flew from her hands, scalding the vines and making them recoil in shock, dropping the fairies.

'But Silky,' Melody objected, 'Petal said —'

'Petal isn't here!' Silky retorted. 'And the plants are fine, which means we only have a minute before they ...'

The vines were way ahead of Silky. Already they had thrown off the shock of her light beam and were inching towards the fairies.

'Fly away!' Silky cried.

The fairies zoomed away at top speed, not caring where they were going as long is it was away from the grasping, clutching vines. They flew past forests of giant clover, their leaves turning like windmills in the breeze. They flew over ponds that looked as if they had pictures drawn on the water ... pictures that were made by millions of multicoloured lilypads.

They flew through clouds of orange, blue and red spores and seeds that clung to their hair and made them look as if they were wearing candyfloss wigs. They flew with no idea where they were going, no way to ask for help and no goal but to somehow find Petal and the Eternal Bloom and get them back to the Faraway Tree.

Suddenly, the fairies stopped short. Their path was blocked by a massive hedge that stretched from ground to sky. Only four openings pierced the hedge's thick foliage: they looked like two wide eyes, a twisted nose and a gaping, grinning, toothy mouth.

'Creepy,' said Melody. 'I think maybe we should turn around.'

'Creepy?' Bizzy challenged. 'It's a Green Growing Grin! It's Great!'

'You know what's *really* great?' Pinx asked, beaming. 'Look at Silky's necklace.'

Silky lifted her crystal pendant. It was glowing a soft pink.

'Yes!' Silky cheered. 'We're close to Petal and the Bloom! We just have to keep going straight.' Silky looked at Melody, who was clearly still uneasy. 'Don't worry, Melody, It'll be OK.'

Melody warily eyed the hedge.

'I don't know,' she said. 'I have a bad feeling about this . . .'

'Oh, come on!' Bizzy said, 'I bet it'll be fun!'

Without another thought, she flew into the grinning mouth, laughingly tapping her finger on the tip of one of its 'teeth' as she flew. Pinx followed close behind. Silky waited and took Melody's hand.

'You're coming, aren't you?' she asked.

Melody gaped one last time at the eerie face gawking out of the bushes, and then sighed and followed Silky through its mouth.

Once inside, Melody had to laugh at herself.

'It's perfectly normal!' she giggled.

It was true. The area beyond the grinning hedge was the least exotic of all the places they'd seen in the Land of Flora. The plants here looked just like the ones growing next to the Faraway Tree. Leaves were green, without wild stripes or polka dots, bark was brown, and although there were flowers of all colours, none was feathered or patterned.

'We're getting closer!' Silky exclaimed, looking at her crystal, which was glowing a deeper pink.

The fairies flew forwards when suddenly, WHOOSH! A large leaf swirled around, scooped them up and plonked them back down where they had begun.

'What was that?' asked Pinx.

'I don't know,' mused Silky. 'Let's try it again.'

They flew forwards, trying to slip past the large-leafed plant.

WHOOSH!

It was no use. The leaf scooped them up again, spun around and dropped them right back where they started.

'Maybe we should go around this plant,' Bizzy suggested.

The others agreed. They soared far to the left of the whirling leaf, but before they could move on . . .

WHOOSH!

A different plant struck this time – a palm with large, sail-like leaves that waved when the fairies approached, fanning a huge wind that sent them tumbling backwards.

'What is going on?' Pinx exclaimed.

'I told you I didn't want to come in here . . .' Melody reminded them.

'That's not very helpful!' snapped Pinx.

'Hey!' Silky said. 'No fighting. If the plants won't let us go past, we'll just turn around and leave. We'll find another way to get through to Petal.'

Silky led the way back to the giant hedge, but as she was about to fly through the mouth, the hedge grew, filling the opening with thorny brambles and stopping Silky in her tracks.

'Up here!' Bizzy called, and tried to fly through the hedge's nose . . . but it filled with branches and spiky leaves as soon as she approached.

'It's not letting us out!' Melody wailed. 'We're going to be stuck here forever!'

'Maybe not,' Bizzy said. 'Maybe they're just Particularly Playful Plants and this is a game of Mere Minor Mischief! I bet if we try to get to Petal again, they'll let us fly right past!'

'I hope so,' Silky said.

She took a deep breath, gritted her teeth and beat her wings hard, boldly leading the others away from the grinning hedge.

'It's working!' Silky cried as they flew past the fan-like palm and the twirling giant-leafed plant. 'We're doing it!'

WHOOSH!

An even bigger palm waved its massive fronds, creating a gust of wind so strong that it sent the fairies tumbling through the air, twisting and turning and flailing ... until they bumped into the super-sticky tongue of a giant Venus Flytrap, and its mouth began to close.

Chapter Seven

An Unwanted Companion

It was the carpet of grass on the ground that first realised the danger. As the cave's other occupant crept towards Petal, the grass tried desperately to warn the fairy. It waved beneath her cheek, her arms and her sides, trying to tickle her awake before it was too late. Petal giggled.

'Mmmmm,' she sighed sleepily.

Slowly, she opened her eyes . . . and screamed at the sight of the hideous Troll looming over her.

'Talon!' Petal gasped.

'Good morning, Petal,' Talon oozed.

The reeking stench of his breath made Petal wince. Talon grabbed her and pulled her closer to him.

'Tell me,' he breathed into her face. 'Who were you talking to before you fell asleep? A certain special plant, perhaps? Maybe the Eternal Bloom?'

Petal was filled with alarm and she trembled as she looked at the Troll. Did Talon know that she could speak to plants?

'I . . . I don't know what you mean,' she stammered.

Thinking fast, she realised that the fact Talon had asked about the Bloom meant that he hadn't seen her.

'Be still,' Petal silently willed the Bloom, and patted her pocket to make sure the Bloom was still safely tucked away.

'You must have heard me talking to my friends,' said Petal.

'Nice try,' sneered Talon, 'but your fellow fairies aren't around. I checked.'

The stomach-turning odour from Talon's mouth made Petal's mind swim, but she forced herself to think. She needed a safe escape plan for herself and the Bloom, and to come up with one, she needed time. She challenged Talon, staring into the blackness of his eyes.

'I'm surprised you're here,' she said. 'I thought you'd still be trapped in the Land of Music.'

Talon cringed at the memory and squeezed Petal so hard that she thought she might snap.

'You have no *idea!*' he roared.

He relaxed his grip slightly. His eyes, however, were still tiny, black pinpricks, and Petal knew that she couldn't let her guard down for an instant.

'I spent all night in that marsh,' Talon growled through gritted teeth. 'All night shoved inside a tube, unable to move an inch, water seeping in and soaking me through. Even my earlobes were wrinkled. In the morning I was accidentally freed by a woodpecker. I won't bore you with the details of what I did to the creatures of the marsh to thank them for my imprisonment . . . but none of them will ever make music again.'

Petal shuddered. Taking the ability to make music from a Land of Music creature was the worst fate imaginable. She could only hope that their friend Allegra would be able to undo whatever Talon had done to those poor instruments.

'I vowed revenge on you and your friends for leaving me in that place,' Talon snarled.

His grip on Petal tightened again, and the hatred in his eyes made her truly frightened for the first time. Moments later he relaxed again, and gave her an evil smile.

'But I'm a reasonable Troll,' he continued, 'and I could be convinced to forgive you . . . *if* you use your powers to help me find the Eternal Bloom.'

Despite her fear, Petal almost laughed out loud.

'Never!' she said. 'I'd never help you steal a Talisman from the Faraway Tree!'

Talon's rotten grin spread even further across his warty face.

'I was hoping you'd say that,' he said, and began to chant a spell in Trollish.

Petal's mind raced. She remembered that Talon's spells could only affect a living creature when he was touching it. She wasn't strong enough to break away from his vice-like grip, but then she saw a vine sitting at the mouth of the cave.

'Help,' she called. 'Help me.'

The vine snaked into the cave at top speed. Swiftly and silently, it wrapped itself around Talon's ankles and yanked hard, jerking the Troll off his feet before he could finish his spell. He fell face-first on to the grassy cave floor, losing his grip on Petal, who quickly

flew away. Her heart was pounding and she knew that Talon would try to grab her again, so she silently asked the vine to tie him up.

The vine tried . . . but as it wound around the Troll, Talon muttered a new incantation in Trollish.

WHOOSH!

Petal turned back at the sound. It couldn't be . . . he couldn't have . . .

But it was. And he had. He had created a massive ball of fire in the middle of the dense growth of plants outside the cave.

'*NO!*' Petal cried.

She clapped her hands to her ears as she was bombarded by terrified screams and howls from the plants. Tortured, Petal sped back to the cave.

'*STOP IT*!' Petal screamed. '*STOP THE FIRE*! Let him go, quickly!'

The vine uncoiled from Talon, who rose and brushed himself off.

'Thank you, Petal,' he said politely, as if she had just passed the scones at tea. 'How nice of you to come back.'

'Stop it, Talon!' Petal screeched. 'Stop the fire! I'll do anything, I'll help you find the Bloom, just please, please, put out the fire *now*!'

Talon bowed.

'My pleasure,' he said. 'But first . . .'

He held out his hand. Everything in Petal wanted to cringe and run away, but she gritted her teeth and placed her hand inside his. Talon smiled as his cold, calloused fingers clamped around hers. He recited a quick spell in Trollish and the fire outside the cave died away. Petal heard joyful shouts and whoops from all the surrounding plants.

'That wasn't so hard, was it?' Talon said. 'I hope you see that as a show of good faith on my part. I could have let the whole Land burn despite your generous offer. And now for your part of the bargain . . .'

Once again, Talon began speaking in Trollish. Soon his crystal lit up in a burst of light, and as it engulfed Petal and she started to lose consciousness, she silently called out once more to her friend the vine, pleading for something she could only hope he understood.

Chapter Eight

The Absolute Worst

'Oh no!' Pinx wailed. 'It's in my hair!'

'It' was a layer of thick, sticky ooze that coated the puffy green pad on which Silky, Melody, Pinx and Bizzy lay tangled. The more they thrashed and tried to escape, the more the slime coated them and the tighter they were held there.

'My cheek is stuck!' Bizzy cried.

'What is this stuff?' Melody asked, attempting to flap a completely glued wing.

'It's how the plant catches its food,' Silky replied, stuck fast on her stomach and fighting to keep her head from the gummy slime. 'Petal would know more than I do, but the glue holds the food tight, until the plant's mouth can close and digest it.'

'Are you saying it's plant spit?' Pinx cried. 'We're covered in plant spit?'

'Swimming in Seas of Sticky Saliva,' Bizzy grimaced.

'But Silky,' Melody said in horror, 'the mouth is almost halfway closed!'

'I know,' Silky replied. 'We don't have much time.'

She concentrated with all her might and tried to fire a beam of light at the plant. Realising what she was doing, the other fairies stopped struggling and watched her. Surely it would work – her light had been their best weapon against the plants before. But it was no use – with her body stuck down so tight, the light couldn't shoot out. Silky felt weak and powerless.

'No way,' Pinx declared. 'I am too special to become plant food.'

She closed her eyes, concentrated . . . and disappeared.

Moments passed, and Silky, Melody and Bizzy exchanged eager glances – had Pinx escaped?

'AAAAAGH!' Pinx roared as she reappeared, even more stuck than before.

Invisibility had no effect at all on the plant's glue.

'I've got it!' Bizzy cried. 'I'll do a spell to get us unstuck!'

She tried to raise her arms in the air, but one of them was stuck tight. She waved the one that was free from the elbow down.

'Bepluck-um muck-um ruckle-cluckle-stuckle-uck!'

'Ba-GAAAK!' clucked a small cockerel, who popped into existence next to the fairies, walked two steps and then got hopelessly stuck in the sludgy goo.

'A cockerel, Bizzy?' Pinx said witheringly.

'*You* try doing a spell when half your mouth is Practically Plastered to a

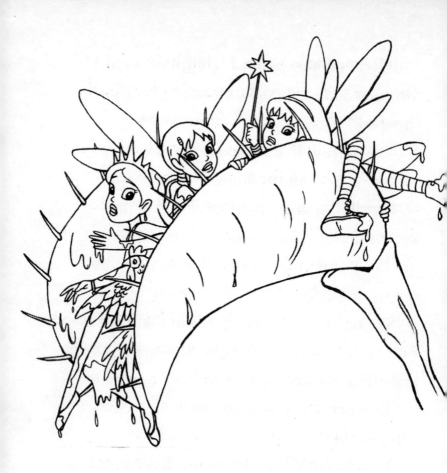

Particularly Peckish Plant!' Bizzy retorted. 'I
suppose that instead of 'unstuck' we got 'one
cluck.'

'Ba-GAAAAAK,' the cockerel agreed.

'My turn,' said Melody.

As the other fairies watched, she

transformed into water . . . but instead of sliding off the plant, she became glued in the sludge, and part of its sticky mess. She transformed into a beautiful dove, but became instantly stuck in the slime. She tried to transform into a rocket that could jet out of the muck, but Melody knew nothing about the mechanics of a real rocket, so she could only transform into a toy model of a rocket, which had no hope of escaping the gluey slop. Again and again Melody transformed herself, but every version of her was just as stuck as the last one. Finally, she went back to herself, completely exhausted from the effort.

'I'm so sorry,' she said softly. 'I thought I could do it, but . . .'

Even Pinx saw how hard Melody was being on herself.

'It's OK, Melody,' she said. 'None of us could.'

'Ba-gaaak,' the bird agreed.

The fairies looked up at the mouth of the plant. It was only feet away from clamping shut and swallowing them forever.

'Then this is it,' Bizzy's voice trembled.

There was a moment of silence and then Pinx cleared her throat.

'Um . . . I know I can be harsh sometimes, but I want you girls to know how much you mean to me –'

'None of that,' Silky snapped. 'Stop it right now.'

'I'm trying to pour my heart out, Silky!' Pinx retorted.

'I'm not letting you!' Silky told her. 'We're not giving up. We need to keep fighting.'

'OK, but can we not fight with each other?' said Melody. 'Please?'

'Fine,' Pinx snapped. 'I won't say a thing; we'll just get eaten and you'll never know how I feel, how's that?'

'Um . . . Pinx? Silky?' Bizzy said.

'Not now, Bizzy,' said Pinx, turning to Silky. 'The next time we're about to lose our lives and *you* want to say something important, don't for a second think I'm going to listen.'

'Hey . . .' Bizzy interjected again, but Pinx and Silky ignored her.

'That doesn't make any sense!' Silky argued.

'It doesn't have to make sense!' Pinx exploded. 'They're my last words; they can be as ridiculous as I want!'

'But they're *not* your last words!' Bizzy cried, 'Look!'

She pointed at the mouth of the Venus Flytrap, which was now held open by the branch of another plant. The mouth strained against the branch, desperate to close and devour its meal, but it couldn't. As the fairies – and the cockerel – watched gratefully, several more branches snaked their way inside the mouth of the Venus Flytrap. Silky, Melody,

Bizzy, Pinx and the cockerel grabbed hold of
a branch each. With a mighty tug, the
branches yanked them to safety, seconds
before the other branch lost its grip and the
Venus Flytrap's mouth snapped tightly shut.

'We're free!' Silky and Pinx cried.

They jumped into each other's arms, their
fight completely forgotten. Melody and Bizzy
joined in the hug and the fairies spun wildly,

laughing and squealing as they flew in a happy circle. Even the cockerel squawked along delightedly before darting off to discover a new life for himself in the Land of Flora.

Silky, Melody, Bizzy and Pinx broke away from their hug and helped each other to clean off the sticky plant slime. They were so excited by their escape that they could have celebrated all day, but the branches that had come to their rescue now tapped them on their shoulders, trying to get their attention. The fairies turned to their rescuers, who urgently shook their leaves.

'I think . . . I think they're trying to tell us something.' Melody said.

'WE – DON'T – SPEAK – PLANT!' Pinx bawled. 'YOU – NEED – TO – HELP – US – UNDERSTAND!'

'They don't know our language, Pinx,' Silky said. 'Speaking loudly and slowly won't change that.'

Silky tried to communicate with body language, shrugging her shoulders and shaking her head to show the plants that the fairies didn't understand.

The branches sagged, clearly disappointed. Then suddenly, a particularly supple branch leaned forwards. Before the fairies' eyes, it bent itself into a clear silhouette of . . .

'PETAL!' Bizzy cried. 'It's a Practically Perfect Petal Picture!'

'Did Petal send you to help us?' asked Melody.

'That makes no sense,' Pinx objected. 'How would Petal know we were in trouble? Or where we were?'

The branches were in action again, all agitatedly pointing their branches, flowers, and leaves in a single direction, and suddenly Silky understood.

'Petal *didn't* know where we were or that we were in trouble,' she realised. 'She sent the plants to find us and bring us back to her . . . which could mean that *Petal's* in trouble!'

'We have to find her,' Melody cried.

Silky nodded to the branches and plants, letting them know that the fairies understood, and were ready to follow their lead.

For what seemed like ages, Silky, Melody, Bizzy and Pinx followed a string of flowers, vines and trees that guided them across the Land of Flora. Finally, they came to the mouth of a beautiful cave beside a stunning waterfall. The matted grass showed clear signs of a struggle.

'Look,' Melody breathed.

The others followed her gaze to an area just outside the cave where a large patch of bushes and flowers was scorched and curled. The fairies now understood the life and vitality of plants more than ever, and their breath caught in their throats as they stared at the blackened husks.

'But how could a fire start here?' Bizzy asked. 'Unless something was struck by lightning . . . but wouldn't that burn more than just this spot?'

A terrible thought was forming in Silky's mind, but she hoped against hope that she was wrong. As she racked her brain to come up with another explanation, a vine tapped her on the shoulder. It slid out of the cave, and Silky followed as far as it could reach. Then it pointed at the opening to a wood, filled with dense foliage. Large sections of the foliage were trampled down and torn.

'Petal would never do that to plants,' Melody said.

'But she's the only thing here apart from us that's not a plant,' Pinx frowned. 'Unless . . .'

Silky nodded. The air seemed to suck out of the Land as she said her terrible thought out loud.

'Talon!'

Chapter Nine

Petal in Peril

As soon as Petal awoke, she struggled to get away from Talon. At least, she tried to struggle, but her body wouldn't listen. Even though she felt a sensation of movement, she was completely paralysed. Fear rushed through her body. Had Talon found the Bloom? Anxiously, she silently called out to her.

'I'm here,' the Bloom's voice whispered in Petal's mind. 'I'm safely tucked away in your pocket. But we do seem to be in a spot of bother, don't we? Are you able to take a look around?'

Although Petal's body was trapped, she could still move her eyes. She looked down and saw an enormous arm around her and felt the feeling of movement: Talon was carrying her tucked under his arm. She gazed further down her body and saw that from her knees down she was buried in soil and packed into a large, hollow stump.

'You *planted* me?' Petal cried indignantly.

'Good morning, my friend,' Talon smiled down at her. 'And yes, I did. Quite clever, if I do say so myself. Don't you agree?'

Petal was too angry to speak.

'Staying silent?' Talon asked. 'I wouldn't do that if I were you. You made me a promise, Petal. You said you'd lead me to the Eternal Bloom. Now start doing whatever you do to talk to the plants and take me to her immediately.'

Petal considered her options. She could ask the plants around her for help, but after the way Talon had started the fire, she didn't dare to put any more plants in danger. She wondered if the vine had understood her last message. Had he been able to get to her friends? No – much as Petal would give anything to see them, she shook the thought out of her head. She had to assume that she was on her own, and somehow find a way for herself and the Bloom to escape. What she needed most was time.

'The best I can do is to ask if any of the plants have seen the Bloom,' she said.

'And I suppose you're waiting for an invitation?' Talon asked angrily. 'Do it! I don't want to be stuck in this wretched Land forever.'

'Calling all plants!' she cried, a ridiculous phrase she would never actually use if she were trying to start a real conversation. 'I'm looking for the Eternal Bloom! Has anyone seen her?'

Hundreds of voices called back to her, most of them speaking to her as if she were quite insane.

'Are you kidding?'

'I thought she was with you?'

'Petal, she's in your *pocket*!'

Petal rolled her eyes. As she pretended to concentrate on listening for a response, she silently explained the situation and asked the plants to spread the word so that she wouldn't have to go over it again and again as she travelled. What she *really* wanted to know, she silently told the plants, was where she could find the most difficult and treacherous parts of the Land of Flora.

'We need to go straight ahead,' Petal finally declared.

Talon's eyes flashed eagerly. 'For how long?' he asked.

'I don't know. I'll ask again when we get closer.'

Talon rushed through the forest, knocking down branches and trampling plants with every step. Petal ached for the creatures he was hurting, but there was nothing she could do about it except silently apologise as they went.

The plants had given Petal excellent information. She and Talon were soon surrounded by thick, thorny brambles that scratched and scraped his skin (but of course refused to harm Petal in any way).

'Are you sure it's this way?' Talon roared, plucking yet another thorn from the tip of his nose.

'Positive,' Petal assured him.

'Fine,' the Troll snapped, 'then I'll just need an axe to make our path a little smoother.'

He began chanting in Trollish, and Petal quickly jumped to the rescue.

'Actually, now the plants are saying we have to go that way!' she exclaimed before he could do any more damage. 'It's not much farther – you can swing on vines to get there!'

Excited, Talon stopped his chanting and quickly swung from vine to vine across the Land of Flora, his feet kicking down smaller plants all along the way.

Eventually Petal could sense that he was getting restless. She directed him towards a small tunnel that was lined by bushes and filled with over-ripe berries.

'You need to go through the tunnel,' Petal told the horrible Troll. 'That's where they're saying she is.'

The tunnel was far too small for Talon, but

he crouched down on his hands and knees
and crawled through.

'Be careful,' Petal warned, pretending to be
helpful. 'The berries are very ripe, and if you
brush against them they might –'

'AAAARRRGH!' Talon wailed.

He was so large that he brushed against
every berry and they all burst, covering him
with sticky juice. Petal was stained as well, but
it was worth it to see Talon when they finally
emerged from the tunnel. He was pink from
head to toe; even his hair had a rosy hue.

Talon gazed around hungrily, aching to grab the Bloom.

'Where is it?' he roared. 'I don't see the Bloom! If you're playing with me . . .'

He looked menacingly down at Petal. She clamped down on the fear that raced through her veins and tried to remain calm.

'I'm not; I promise,' she lied. 'The Bloom has friends in the Land. They move her around.'

'Lead me to her friends,' Talon growled. 'I'll destroy them.'

'No!' Petal cried. 'Just let me explain the situation.'

She took a deep breath, then cried out, 'Calling all plants! Talon the Troll is serious. He needs to find the Bloom *now*. No more games: tell me where she is!'

Petal listened not for directions to the Bloom, but for the answer to her silent request: directions to something that might make Talon drop her, so that she and the Bloom could escape. It wasn't a great plan, but at that moment it was all she could do.

At last she received the answer she wanted.

'The Bloom isn't far,' she told Talon. 'Just a little way down this path.'

Talon followed Petal's directions, thrashing plants all the way, until at last he came to a patch of thick plants that looked almost like a giant octopus, with large tentacles waving in the air.

'Tunnelling Banshee Plants,' Petal explained to Talon. 'They're hiding the Bloom in their tunnels. Pull one of them out and you'll find the Bloom.'

Talon's sickening grin spread wider than ever across his face.

'Thank you, Petal,' he said. 'You've been most helpful.'

Keeping Petal tucked under his arm, Talon reached down, grabbed several tentacles of the nearest Banshee Plant, and pulled . . .

'AAAAAAHHHHHH!'

It was the scream of the Banshee Plant, which was actually known as the *Wailing* Banshee Plant, not the *Tunnelling* Banshee Plant. The Banshee was well known among nature lovers for the ear-splitting scream it produced when uprooted, and its ability to replant itself when thrown away.

Talon reeled at the sound of the Banshee's hideous screech and threw the offending plant as far away as he could. What he did not do, however, was lose his grip on Petal. He held her up in front of him, his pink-stained face now red with rage.

'ENOUGH!' he screamed at her. 'You think this is a game? You think you can toy with me? You told me that plants can move the Bloom. You have exactly ten seconds to get them to bring it to me, or I'll start another fire . . . and throw you right in the middle of it! Ten . . . Nine . . .'

Petal's terrified mind raced as Talon
continued his brutal countdown. What was
she going to do?

Chapter Ten

A Way Out?

'Seven . . . Six . . .' roared Talon.

Petal's heart raced. What was she going to do? She couldn't give Talon the Bloom, but if he really did start a fire and throw Petal in, wouldn't the Bloom perish right along with her?

'Petal, it's OK,' cried the Bloom. 'Save yourself. Give me to him.'

It wasn't the first time the Bloom had said this to Petal, but Petal's response was always the same. Absolutely not. She would find a way to save them. Somehow . . . somehow . . .

'Three . . . Two . . .' boomed Talon.

'Stop, Talon!' cried an unmistakable voice.

Petal almost burst into tears of joy when she saw Silky, Melody, Pinx and Bizzy. Talon looked up as well, and even in these dangerous circumstances, his pink skin and hair took the fairies by surprise.

'Wow, Talon,' Pinx said with a grin, 'you look fantastic! If we weren't going to completely flatten you before we leave, I'd put you into my next fashion show!'

'My appearance is unimportant,' sneered Talon, 'as are you. Your friend can't move; she's completely at my mercy. Make one false move and I'll destroy her. Now if you'll excuse me, Petal and I were in the middle of something.'

As Talon gleefully told the fairies his plan, Petal began to smile. She had an idea. She had never tried it before, but she somehow knew deep inside that it would work. She concentrated on her friends in the same way that she concentrated on plants and animals when she wanted to speak to them without making a sound.

'Whatever you do, do not react to the
sound of my voice,' Petal's voice said in the
other fairies' heads.

Bizzy's jaw dropped and Melody gasped.

'I see you're impressed,' Talon said, grinning
wickedly. 'As well you should be. And don't
think I won't do it. Petal could tell you about
what happened earlier . . .'

Thankfully, Talon thought that Bizzy and Melody were reacting to *him*, and so he began to gloat about the fire he had made earlier.

Bizzy and Melody wiped the telltale reactions off their faces and subtly caught the eyes of Pinx and Silky. Immediately, they all understood that they were hearing the same thing in their heads. They outwardly pretended to concentrate on Talon's bragging tale of his own power, but their real attention was on Petal's voice.

'I have a plan, and I need you to listen carefully, because there will be no time to repeat it,' she said. 'Melody, at the last minute, when Talon thinks he's won, sing "Now" in your loudest voice. When you hear that, Silky, use your light to blind Talon for a moment. He'll automatically let go of me to grab his eyes, and Pinx, when he does, you must become invisible and grab me. Keep me upright; the Eternal Bloom is in my pocket.

The second I'm free, I'll ask the plants to make a cage around Talon. When I do that, Bizzy, I need you to do a spell to cover it with meteors.'

'Meteors?' Bizzy exclaimed aloud, stopping Talon's story in its tracks.

He stared at her while Pinx, Silky and Melody glared – what was she doing? Bizzy cleared her throat and tried to cover.

'Me . . . see . . . yours,' she stammered to Talon. 'Your point, that is. I see your point.'

'Thank you,' Talon oozed. 'If you have no further interruptions, I'd like to pick up where we left off.' He cast his eyes down at Petal. 'You know the rules, Petal. I believe you had two more seconds. Two . . .'

Petal looked completely impassive, giving no sign of what she hoped was to come. The other fairies exchanged glances: it was time for action.

'. . . One!' Talon roared.

'NOW!' Melody sang out in her loudest voice.

Silky shot a beam of light into Talon's eyes, blinding him before he could start another magical fire.

Just as Petal knew he would, the Troll grabbed at his eyes, releasing Petal, who was scooped up by an invisible Pinx just as Talon's vision returned.

He grabbed for Petal, but she had already been concentrating with all her might, using her power to call on dozens of thick, thorny plants, who promptly rose around Talon in a tight, prickly cage.

By the time the cage was around the Troll, Bizzy had already begun her spell to make the meteors.

'Meetey-oo, meetleodle, mizzoo, mizzoh, mizzleizzle!'

She thrust her arms forwards and instantly the inside of the cage was covered with . . .

Mirrors.

Not meteors, mirrors.

Hundreds of different mirrors, each in its own ornate frame.

Bizzy had messed up the spell.

Chapter Eleven

The Farewell

Bizzy gasped, horrified by her mistake.

'No!' she cried. 'Not mirrors! I meant meteors!'

She was sure that she had ruined everything and Talon would race out to destroy them all. Talon roared a spell in Trollish and his crystal flashed in a burst of enchanted light . . .

But the spell-light merely bounced off the mirrors that covered the inside of the cage!

'NO!' raged Talon.

He tore at the mirrors, but because they were enchanted, they stuck tightly to the cage walls and didn't break when he kicked and punched them. As for the thorny cage bars, the lining of mirrors meant that Talon couldn't get his hands on them, so they too were saved from his fury. Talon was completely helpless.

'Actually,' Melody noted, 'it looks as if your mistake worked out for the best.'

'Imagine that,' Silky said knowingly, catching Petal's eye and smiling.

Bizzy heard the laughter in Silky's voice.

'Imagine what?' she cried. 'What are you talking about? I messed up the spell! Didn't I?'

'Actually,' Petal explained, still planted in her pot and standing next to Pinx, 'I *wanted* the cage covered with mirrors. I was sort of counting on a Basic Bizzy Blunder.'

Bizzy's face flushed as she stammered for the right response.

'You ... How dare ... I've never ...'

Petal winced, feeling awful for offending her friend, but within moments Bizzy was laughing out loud, her curls bobbing as she gave a big shrug.

'Hey, it worked!' she declared. 'That makes it the Biggest Best Bizzy Blunder there's ever been!'

'Brilliant!' Petal grinned.

Bizzy ran to give her a hug, but she toppled Petal over into Pinx, who caught her before she hit the ground.

'Ooooh, sorry,' Bizzy winced.

'So what do we do about this?' asked Pinx, pushing Petal upright once again. 'I know you love plants, but I don't think you want to *be* one.'

'I have a plan for that, too,' Petal said, and turned her eyes back to Bizzy. 'Think you can do it?' she asked.

'Do what?' Bizzy asked.

Petal just kept looking at her, and Bizzy realised what she meant. Her eyes grew wide with amazement.

'You mean . . . you want me to magic you back to normal?' she asked.

'That's exactly what I mean,' Petal answered. 'And if you could give me a little extra energy while you're at it, that would be great. That cage took a lot out of me.'

'But . . . I always mess up my spells,' Bizzy objected. 'You counted on it to trap Talon. Big Blunders are Basic Bizzy Business.'

'Yeah, Petal,' Pinx jumped in. 'Are you sure you want to –'

'I'm sure,' Petal said, not taking her eyes off Bizzy. 'I believe Bizzy can do it. And if you really think about it, I bet the rest of you do, too.'

Melody, Silky and Pinx exchanged glances. *Did* they believe Bizzy could do it? They really weren't sure, but this didn't seem like the time to say so.

'Sure,' said Silky.

'Of course we do,' Melody smiled.

'Yeah, I mean, if I really think about it . . .' Pinx added.

Petal looked meaningfully at Bizzy.

'I need you, Bizzy,' she said. 'Will you help me?'

Bizzy bit her bottom lip and then nodded. She raised her arms above her head, letting her bracelets rattle to her elbows. She closed her eyes and concentrated.

'Unstickle-ickle, mover-dee-dickle, mosha-gosha-ohsha-loo!'

Bizzy flung out her arms in Petal's direction, and for several moments no one breathed. Bizzy refused to open her eyes, terrified of what she might see.

'Bizzy?'

Bizzy opened her eyes. Petal was standing in front of her, a huge grin on her face.

'You're out of the pot!' Bizzy cried. 'You moved out of the pot! It worked! You're a Perfectly Potless Petal!'

She threw her arms around Petal, who gratefully hugged her back.

'I knew you could do it,' Petal said.

'Well, yes. We all knew you could do it,' Pinx added.

'Or at least we know it now,' Silky amended, beaming as she threw her arms around Bizzy. 'You're amazing.'

'RAAAAAAAHHHHHH!' A roar of wild fury came from Talon's cage as he tried to escape.

'Maybe we should celebrate somewhere else,' Melody suggested.

The others agreed, and Silky led the way towards the Ladder and home. They all breathed a sigh of relief when they saw that the Ladder was still there, but before they could climb down to the Faraway Tree, Petal looked at them sadly.

'This is where we have to say goodbye,' she said.

Silky, Pinx, Bizzy and Melody stopped in their tracks, stunned.

'What are you talking about?' said Pinx. 'You're coming home with us. Let's go.'

Petal held her ground.

'I can't,' she said. 'I promised the Eternal Bloom that she would never have to go back to the Vault.'

'This again?' Pinx exploded. 'We're not letting the plant decide what we're doing!'

Silky held up a hand to silence Pinx.

'The Bloom is a living creature, just like us,' she said. 'If she really doesn't want to go back, we have to respect that.'

'Fine,' Bizzy said, turning to Petal, 'but that doesn't mean *you* can't come home. We'll just find a Perfect Plot for her Hidden Hideout!'

Petal smiled, but shook her head.

'Nowhere would be safe enough,' she said. 'Not with Talon here, desperate for Talismans. She needs someone to protect her.'

'But if you stay and the Bloom's not in the Vault, the Land of Flora won't be tied to the Faraway Tree any more,' said Melody. 'You'll never be able to come back home.'

Despite herself, tears started to well in Petal's eyes.

'I know,' she said.

'No!' Melody objected, fighting back her own tears. 'You're not leaving us again! It's not right: you don't abandon your friends.'

'Oh, Melody,' Petal began, reaching out to

hug her friend. 'I'm so sorry I ran away from everyone before; I shouldn't have done that. But this is different; there's no other way.'

'Then we'll stay with you!' Melody declared.

'If we did that, who would find the Talismans and save the Faraway Tree?' Silky asked quietly.

They knew that she was right. Petal was staying, and Silky, Pinx, Melody and Bizzy needed to go.

'I don't accept it,' Pinx said. 'There has to be another way.'

She stood defiantly with her hands on her hips, but tears welled in her eyes.

'I love you too, Pinx,' Petal said through her tears.

She hugged Pinx and then looked her in the eye.

'I always looked up to you for your strength,' she said. 'Even when we were kids.'

Pinx choked out a laugh. 'You're so much stronger than I am. I'd be going home with the rest of us.'

'You wouldn't,' Petal said knowingly.

She squeezed Pinx's hands and then flew to Melody.

'It's not right,' Melody sniffled. 'Friends shouldn't have to leave each other.'

'Real friends never do,' said Petal. 'We'll always be together in our hearts.'

Melody nodded, and she and Petal threw their arms around one another.

'Every night when I go to sleep, I'll imagine you singing to me,' Petal assured her. 'It's the most beautiful lullaby in the whole Enchanted World.'

They slowly pulled away from one another, and Petal flew to Bizzy.

'Hi, crazy fairy,' Petal said, and they both laughed despite the tears slipping down their cheeks.

'I feel as if I should have something Supremely Sentimental to say,' Bizzy began, 'but I can't find any words.'

'You?' Petal cried. 'Not a chance.'

'You believed in me,' said Bizzy, becoming serious. 'I didn't even believe in myself, but you believed in me.'

'You heard what Silky said: you're amazing,' said Petal. 'Don't ever forget it.'

Petal pulled Bizzy close and they hugged. Finally, Petal flew to Silky.

'I don't even know what to say to you,' Petal began, her voice cracking. 'It's all your fault I fell in with this lot to begin with.'

'And you told me you were afraid you could never leave Fairyland,' Silky reminded her. 'Now look at you.'

Her voice trembled and tears filled her eyes.

'Petal,' she stammered, 'I promise you, if I had had any idea it would come to this, I would never have –'

'Stop,' Petal insisted. 'The four of you are the best things that ever happened to me. I wouldn't change our time together for the entire Enchanted World.'

Petal flew back, looking at all her friends.

'I love you girls,' she said simply. 'I'm going to miss you all so much.'

That did it. Any last bit of composure any of them had melted away, and the five best friends sobbed together as they fell into each other's arms, letting their tears flow freely as they prepared to go their separate ways forever.

Chapter Twelve

A Special Surprise

Silky was the first to start back down the Ladder. Heartbreaking as it was to even consider leaving Petal behind, Silky felt that she should be the one to lead the way. But just as her feet flitted past the top rung . . .

'STOP!' Petal cried.

'What is it?' Silky asked.

The fairies turned to see Petal pull the Eternal Bloom from her pocket.

'That's what the Bloom said,' Petal explained. 'She screamed "Stop!" and told me to shout it out to all of you.'

Petal's eyes widened as she stared at the Bloom, listening. Then she looked back at her friends.

'She's crying,' Petal told them.

Petal listened to the Bloom again and frowned.

'Are you sure?' she asked the flower.

Again Petal listened, and at last she nodded. Fresh tears welled in her eyes as she turned back to her friends.

'What's wrong? What did she say?' Melody asked.

'The Bloom said that after hearing everything we were willing to sacrifice for her, she's ready to make a sacrifice too,' Petal said. 'She wants to go back to the Vault.'

'But she hated it there,' Bizzy protested.

'I know,' Petal agreed. 'But she says it's where she belongs.'

'Is she sure?' Pinx asked.

Petal smiled. 'Are you worried about her?'

'No!' Pinx retorted. 'I'm just saying, she was so sure it would be the worst thing in the world down there for her ... I just want to make sure she knows what she's doing.'

'She says she does,' Petal answered simply. 'She says it's better for her to go back there than for me to be stuck here. I told her it's OK, I'm happy to stay here for her . . . but she says she won't allow it.'

'So . . . you're really coming back with us?' Melody asked.

Petal smiled. 'I really am.'

The fairies flew together for a huge hug, and then Melody, Bizzy and Pinx flew down the Ladder, eager to get back home to the Faraway Tree.

Before Silky followed them, she crouched down so that she was level with the Eternal Bloom.

'Thank you,' she said. 'You've given us a greater gift than you could ever imagine.'

She kissed the Bloom tenderly and then turned to Petal.

'We'll meet you in the Tree,' she said.

Silky flew down the Ladder, leaving Petal

to give the Bloom one final moment of freedom in the Land of Flora.

'Your friends are truly special, Petal,' the Bloom sighed.

'All my friends are,' Petal replied, 'including you.'

The Bloom took one final look around the Land of Flora.

'I really loved it here,' she said wistfully. 'I'll truly miss it.'

'It's not too late to change your mind,' Petal assured her. 'No one would blame you if –'

'Don't say it,' cried the Bloom. 'I know my place. I was chosen to be a Talisman and live in the Vault. You chose to follow your dreams. For me to stand in your way because of a selfish desire to be more than I am . . . it isn't right, Petal, and I won't let it happen. Come now – I don't want to be here one more second. Take me back to the Vault.'

Petal ached to ask her once more if she was sure, but the fairy already knew the answer. Gently cradling the Bloom in her hand, she turned her back on the Land of Flora and flew down the Ladder.

She didn't stop until she reached the door of the Vault, where Witch Whisper and the other fairies were already waiting for her.

Pinx, Silky, Melody and Bizzy gathered around Petal, knowing how difficult this would be for her.

'I'll always remember your sacrifice, my friend,' Petal told the Bloom in a trembling voice. 'Thank you.'

As Petal kissed the Bloom, Witch Whisper looked confused.

'Sacrifice?' Witch Whisper asked.

'The greatest sacrifice,' Petal explained. 'The Bloom hates the Vault. She wants to be free. She's only going back for us.'

Petal held the Bloom out to Witch Whisper, who took her from Petal's hands. Immediately, Petal turned and flew back towards the fairies' home high above. Her friends followed, leaving Witch Whisper holding the Bloom to her own face, and giving it a very curious look indeed.

Three days later, Pinx burst into Petal's room with Melody, Pinx and Silky. Petal was lying in her garden, staring up at the Tree's branches.

'That's it!' Pinx announced as she soared down to her friend. 'No more moping! You haven't even moved for three days! Little woodland creatures are barging into *my* room. I don't *like* little woodland creatures in my room, Petal!'

'They mostly want food,' Petal said distractedly. 'Give them a muffin and they'll leave you alone.'

'That's not the point!' Pinx cried.

Silky flew down and sat cross-legged next to Petal.

'Pinx means that she's worried about you,' she said. 'We all are.'

'Why don't you come out for a little while?' Bizzy suggested. 'Just to the kitchen. I can make some Magic Message Muffins!'

'No, thanks,' Petal said. 'I'm not hungry.'

'You know, Petal,' Melody began gently, 'this isn't what the Bloom would have wanted for you.'

'I know,' Petal conceded. 'I just can't stop thinking about her trapped in that Vault . . . it's not fair.'

'Sometimes things in life aren't fair,' said a voice from above.

The fairies looked up to see a figure soaring towards them, the folds of her cloak billowing around her.

'Witch Whisper,' Petal said, standing up.

'But sometimes . . .' Witch Whisper continued, '. . . they are.'

She held out her hands. Cupped inside was . . .

'The Bloom!' Petal cried.

She reached out and took the flower from Witch Whisper, then started to laugh.

'Stop, stop!' she giggled to the Bloom, 'You're talking so fast, even I can't understand!'

'Maybe I can explain,' Witch Whisper said. 'I didn't put the Bloom back into the Vault. She has been with me in my cottage the last three days. I've been thinking about what you said. When those of us who created the Vault chose items to be the Talismans, we thought of them as inanimate objects. A feather, a harp . . . a flower.'

'But a flower's alive,' Petal said.

'We knew that, of course,' said Witch Whisper, 'but none of us had your skills, Petal. We had no idea *how* alive it was, how complex its thoughts and feelings could be. But when you told me how much the Bloom dreaded going back into the Vault, and how she volunteered to do it anyway as a sacrifice for her friends . . . she's as alive as any of us. I couldn't forgive myself if I locked her up forever.'

Petal couldn't believe her ears.

'What about the Faraway Tree's life force?' she asked. 'Or keeping the Tree tied to the other Lands? I thought the Talismans had to be in the Vault to –'

Witch Whisper shook her head.

'The Talismans just need to be in the Tree,' she explained. 'The Vault is the safest place for most of them, but in the Bloom's case, I think she would be better off somewhere more familiar . . . in a garden, perhaps . . .'

'You mean she can stay with *me*?' Petal threw her arms around Witch Whisper. 'Thank you! Thank you so much!'

'I can't think of anywhere safer than with you girls watching her,' Witch Whisper declared. 'Of course, when you're all on your missions . . .'

'Zuni and Misty can watch her!' Silky suggested. 'They'd be happy to, I know it!'

'Then it's settled,' said Witch Whisper. 'All that's left is to introduce our new friend to all her new neighbours in the tree.'

Pinx's eyes widened.

'A party!' she cried. 'I'll handle the decorations: red, in honour of our new housemate!'

'I can choose the music!' Melody chimed in.

'I'll make the food!' Bizzy offered. 'New
Neighbour Nachos!'

'I'll spread the word!' Silky volunteered.
'The Bloom will get to meet everyone!'

As Petal's friends raced off to get ready for
the party, Witch Whisper winked at Petal.

'I'll leave you two to catch up,' she said,
making her way through the garden towards
the rest of the Tree. 'See you tonight!'

'So what do you think?' Petal asked the Bloom when they were alone. 'Would you like to live here with me in the garden?'

'Oh Petal, is it really true?' the Bloom asked. 'I can stay with you, and I don't ever have to go back to the Vault again?'

'Never,' Petal promised her. 'Welcome home.'

That night, everyone who lived in the Faraway Tree came to meet their newest neighbour. The Bloom, with Petal's help as translator, spoke to each and every guest. The party was a spectacular success. It reminded Petal how much she loved life in the Faraway Tree, and how terribly close she had come to losing it. But even as she celebrated, she knew that it was only a matter of time before a new Land settled at the top of the Tree, sending Petal and her friends on another adventure into the unknown.

Petal grinned. Let the next Land come. As long as she was with her four best friends, she could handle anything.

If you can't wait for another exciting
adventure with Silky and her fairy
friends, here's a sneak preview . . .

Enid Blyton's
ENCHANTED
WORLD
Pinx and the
Ring of Midnight

For fun and activities, go to
www.blyton.com/enchantedworld

Chapter One

Faraway Tree Makeovers

'Voila!' Pinx crowed, standing back to admire her work. 'Tell me that doesn't look magnificent!' Pinx bent down to her customer and added, 'That's just a figure of speech. Don't even dream of actually telling me it doesn't look magnificent.'

The Angry Pixie studied himself in the mirror. His pinched face frowned as he inspected his new look. His goatee beard was dyed purple and plaited with shining strips of light pink fabric; his bald head was covered by a gold-and-red beaded turban, festooned with giant feathers that cascaded over his forehead; his moustache was twisted at the ends and dipped in hot pink wax.

He frowned. He tilted his head first to one

side and then to the other. He fingered the waxy tips of his moustache. Then he raised an eyebrow.

'I like it,' he declared. 'I look . . . fancy.'

He stood up and struck a dignified pose.

'Thank you, Pinx,' he said. 'Thank you very much.'

'My pleasure,' said Pinx. 'And yours, of course.'

As Pinx packed up her supplies and flitted out of the Angry Pixie's home, she called back, 'Remember: "If it's not by Pinx . . ."'

'. . . your makeover stinks!"' finished the Angry Pixie.

Pinx flew home, keeping an eye out for any creatures whose looks she thought she could improve. Life in the Faraway Tree was so much more *fun* now that she had started her new project!

It had all begun a few weeks earlier, soon after Pinx and her friends had successfully returned from the Land of Flora. Ever since Pinx had moved to the Faraway Tree, she had kept herself busy with fun fashion and style challenges, such as redecorating the fairies' treehouse so that everything was upside down. Things like this were fun, but they couldn't compare to the thrill of designing outfits for huge parties like Princess Twilleria's Sweet Centennial, or Duchess Eleanorian's Birthday Ball. Pinx craved something big into which she could sink her teeth.

Finally, inspiration had struck in the form of the most hideous colour clash imaginable. Elf Riverflower – one of the elves who guarded the Vault – darted past Pinx on her way to work, wearing drab olive clothes and carrying a shockingly bright lime wand.

Oh no. Not in Pinx's Tree.

Pinx had pulled Riverflower into her room and refused to let her leave until she was outfitted with twelve spectacular wand-covers, each a perfect match for a fabulous new Pinx-designed outfit, complete with ruffellettas, bubbloons, bells and whistles. Tree residents could hear Riverflower coming from a mile away, and in no time everyone was jealously buzzing about her exciting new look and the amazingly talented fairy behind it. Pinx was in her element again, and it felt phenomenal.

From that moment on, Pinx was inspired. She constantly searched the Faraway Tree for fashion mistakes. As soon as she saw one, she pounced with a cry of, 'Congratulations! You've just earned a Faraway Tree Makeover!' The lucky recipient was always pleased with the result, just like the Angry Pixie; and Pinx was always thrilled to work her makeover magic.

As soon as Pinx soared back into the fairies' large main room, she realised that there would be no more makeovers for a while. The room was as full as it had ever been, most of its space occupied by the hunched-over figure of Gino the Giant. He was nursing a bad cold, and dabbed at his nose with a lacy pink handkerchief, an accessory from his recent Pinx makeover. Silky, Melody, Bizzy and Petal were squashed into the remaining space with Witch Whisper and Cluecatcher. That could only mean one thing . . .

'There's a new Land at the top of the Tree!' Silky called excitedly.

'Great,' said Pinx, trying to echo Silky's enthusiasm.

The truth was that Pinx wasn't sure how she felt about going up into another Land. She was flawless at makeovers, but there were times during the Faraway Fairies' missions that she doubted whether she was doing as much for the team as some of the others. Melody had transformed herself into Queen

Quadrille to outsmart Talon the Troll in the Land of Music. Silky was a brave and quick-thinking leader. Petal had saved her friends by communicating with the flowers in the Land of Flora. Even Bizzy's muddled spells seemed to work out brilliantly in the end. But Pinx . . .

Pinx pushed those thoughts out of her head. She prided herself on being fearless. She could barely admit her worries to herself; she certainly wasn't going to let the others see how she felt.

'So which Land is it?' Pinx asked in the most excited voice she could muster. 'Where are we going next?'

'AAAHHH!' cried Cluecatcher.

All eight of his eyes widened, and his super-sensitive radar dish ears clapped down on his head at the volume of Pinx's exclamation.

'The Land of Giants,' said Witch Whisper, amused by Pinx's enthusiasm.

'My homeland,' added Gino. 'It's so beautiful. I wish I could go with you, but . . . ah . . . ah . . . ah . . . AHHCHOOO!'

His thundering sneeze rocked the room. Witch Whisper waited for the wind to die down and then continued.

'The Land of Giants' Talisman is the Ring of Midnight,' she said. 'It is large enough to fit on the finger of a male giant, with a central stone of the blackest onyx surrounded by diamonds as sparkling as the stars themselves. Not only does it startle everyone with its beauty, but the Ring gives its wearer a sense of absolute power and confidence. If a giant has this prize on his finger, it won't be easy for you to take it back.'

'Especially if it's a Gigante giant,' Gino added.

'What's a Gigante giant?' asked Silky.

'I hope you never have to find out,' Gino said. 'They're terrible.'

He looked around, as if afraid that a Gigante giant might be within earshot at that very moment. Then he leaned in closer to the fairies.

'There are two kinds of giant in the Land of Giants,' he said, 'There are the Grande giants and the Gigante giants. You can always tell them apart. Grande giants have a ring-shaped mole on their right cheek; Gigante giants have a ring-shaped mole on their left cheek.'

Gino pointed to his own right cheek, on which there was indeed a ring-shaped mole. He was clearly a Grande giant.

'Never forget the difference,' he warned them.

'What *is* the difference?' Bizzy asked. 'I mean, other than the mole.'

'What's the difference?' Gino squeaked.

It was an odd, frightened sound coming from someone so large. The fairies would have laughed if Gino hadn't looked so serious.

'Grande giants are kind, loving, and generous,' he explained, 'but Gigante giants are bloodthirsty and brutal. They'd rather rip you to shreds than say hello. They're awful! Will you promise me that you will do exactly what the Grande giants do and stay far, far away from any Gigantes?'

'We'll try,' said Petal. 'But what if the Ring is with a Gigante?'

The thought was clearly too terrible for Gino to bear. His eyes widened in shock and then filled with tears. He pulled all five fairies into his arms and hugged them.

'Let's just hope really hard that it's not, OK?' he said with a sob.

After several moments had passed and the fairies were still clutched in Gino's desperate embrace, Witch Whisper cleared her throat.

'We all appreciate your concern, Gino,' she said, 'but it is vital that the fairies make their way up the Ladder.'

Reluctantly, Gino loosened his grip on the fairies, all of whom were too overwhelmed by Gino's fears even to speak. As they flew out of his arms, he locked eyes with each one of them.

'Be safe,' he said. 'Just promise me you'll be safe.'

'I'm sure they will, Gino,' said Witch Whisper. 'Thank you for your help.'

She turned to the fairies.

'I believe that you now have all the information you need,' she told them. 'Good luck. We await your successful return.'

The fairies were unusually silent as they flew up to the Ladder at the top of the Tree, stopping along the way to drop off the Eternal Bloom with Zuni and Misty, who would look after her while the fairies were away. (As the only living Talisman to be recovered by the fairies, the Eternal Bloom did not live in the Vault. Instead, she lived with the folk of the Faraway Tree and was guarded at all times by at least one of the residents.)

The fairies could not get Gino's emotional farewell out of their minds. When they finally reached the bottom rung of the Ladder, they paused and looked nervously at each other. Pinx tried to lift their mood.

'Good thing I'm with you lot on this one,' she said. 'If there's one thing I know, it's beautiful jewellery. Of course, we all know there's far more than *one* thing I know . . .'

Her sentence trailed off. After what they had heard from Gino, Pinx was not at all confident that anything she could offer would be truly helpful on this mission. She had been waiting for her chance to shine, but now she was worried that this challenge would be too big.

'When Gino said that the Gigante giants would rather rip us to shreds than say hello, that was just a figure of speech, wasn't it?' said Melody.

The fairies had seen the look on Gino's face when he had said it; none of them believed it was just a figure of speech. Still, they had no desire to admit that out loud.

'Let's just hope the Ladder leads to the Grande giants,' Silky said, 'and that they're the ones who have the Ring.'

Silky looked up towards the top of the Ladder, shrouded by clouds that completely hid whatever dangers awaited them.

'There's only one way to find out,' said Pinx.

She took a deep breath, stepped on to the Ladder and led her friends through the clouds and into the unknown.

EGMONT PRESS: ETHICAL PUBLISHING

Egmont Press is about turning writers into successful authors and children into passionate readers – producing books that enrich and entertain. As a responsible children's publisher, we go even further, considering the world in which our consumers are growing up.

Safety First
Naturally, all of our books meet legal safety requirements. But we go further than this; every book with play value is tested to the highest standards – if it fails, it's back to the drawing-board.

Made Fairly
We are working to ensure that the workers involved in our supply chain – the people that make our books – are treated with fairness and respect.

Responsible Forestry
We are committed to ensuring all our papers come from environmentally and socially responsible forest sources.

For more information, please visit our website at
www.egmont.co.uk/ethicalpublishing

The Forest Stewardship Council (FSC) is an international, non-governmental organisation dedicated to promoting responsible management of the world's forests. FSC operates a system of forest certification and product labelling that allows consumers to identify wood and wood-based products from well-managed forests.

For more information about the FSC, please visit their website at www.fsc-uk.org

Mixed Sources
Product group from well-managed forests and other controlled sources
Cert no. TT-COC-002332
www.fsc.org
© 1996 Forest Stewardship Council